LUCKY LUKE

DALTON CITY

TEXT BY GOSCINNY   DRAWINGS BY MORRIS

TRANSLATED BY FREDERICK W NOLAN

GLO'WORM

LUCKY LUKE THROUGHOUT THE WORLD

AUSTRIA	Delta Verlag, Postfach 10 12 45, 70011 Stuttgart, Germany
BELGIUM	EDL-B&M S.A., 7 Avenue Paul Henri Spaak, 1060 Brussels, Belgium
CANADA	Diffusion du Livre Mirabel, 5757 rue Cypihot, St. Laurent, QC, H4S 1R3, Canada (French language Distribution)
CROATIA	Izvori Publishing House, Trnjanska 47, 4100 Zagreb, Croatia
CZECH REPUBLIC	United Fans, AS, ul. 5 Kvetna 64, Prague 4, Czech Republic
DENMARK	Carlsen Comics, Krogshøjvej 32, 2880 Bagsvaerd, Denmark
ESTONIA	Egmont Estonia Ltd., Hobujaama 1, EE 0001 Tallinn, Estonia
FINLAND	Otava, Uudenmaankatu 8-12, Helsinki, Finland
FRANCE	Dargaud Editeur, 6 rue Gager Gabillot, 75015 Paris, France
GERMANY	Delta Verlag, Postfach 10 12 45, 70011 Stuttgart, Germany
GREECE	Mamouth Comix Ltd., Solonos 130, 10681 Athens, Greece
HOLLAND	EDL-B&M SA., 7 Avenue Paul Henri Spaak, 1060 Brussels, Belgium (Distribution : Betapress, Burg. Krollaan 14, 5126 PT Jilze, Holland)
INDIA	Shishu Sahitya Samsad Pvt. Ltd., 32A Acharya Prafulla Chandra Road, Calcutta 700 009, India (Bengali and English)
INDONESIA	Pt. Indira, Jalan Borobudur 20, Jakarta 10320, Indonesia
REPUBLIC OF KOREA	Cosmos Editions, 19-16 Shin An-dong, Jin Ju, Gyung Nam-do, Republic of Korea
LATIN AMERICA	Grijalbo-Dargaud, Aragon 385, 08013 Barcelona, Spain
NORWAY	Egmont Serieforlaget, 0055 Oslo, Norway
PORTUGAL	Meriberica-Liber, Av. Duque d'Avila 26 - 5°, 1000 Lisbon, Portugal
SPAIN	Grijalbo-Dargaud, Aragon 385, 08013 Barcelona, Spain
SWEDEN	Bonnier Carlsen Bokförlag, Box 1315, 111 83 Stockholm, Sweden
SWITZERLAND	Dargaud (Suisse) S.A., En Budron B-13, 1052 Le Mont/Lausanne, Switzerland
TURKEY	Dogan Egmont Yayancilik AS, Dogan Holding AS, Dogan Medya Center, 34554 Bagcilar-Istambul, Turkey
UNITED KINGDOM	Glo'worm, 17 Lansdowne Road, London E18 2AZ, Great Britain (Worldwide English-language distribution, excluding the Indian sub-continent)
VIETNAM	Tre Publishing House, 161B Ly Ching Thang, 3rd District, Ho Chi Minh City, Socialist Republic of Vietnam
YUGOSLAV FEDERATION	NIP Politika - Politikin Zabavnik,Makedonska 29, 11000 Belgrade, Yugoslav Federation

© Dargaud Editeur Paris 1969 by Morris and Goscinny

A CIP catalogue record for this book is available from the British Library.

ISBN : 1 902172 01 9

1998 Published by GLO'WORM
Exclusive English language publisher of Lucky Luke throughout the world
(excluding the Indian sub-continent)

GLO'WORM is a trade imprint of Cottleston Books Limited of
17, Lansdowne Road, London E18 2AZ, England.
Web address: www.cottleston.demon.co.uk
Cottleston Books Limited is a subsidiary of Cottleston Limited

Printed in France by PPO-93500 Pantin

ENTON TOWN HAD WON, HANDS DOWN, THE SAD REPUTATION OF BEING THE MOST DEPRAVED TOWN IN TEXAS. SALOONS, GAMBLING HOUSES AND SEEDY HOTELS COMPRISED THE LARGER PART OF THE PLACE, WHICH ATTRACTED ANY OUTLAWS IN SEARCH OF AMUSEMENT OR LOOKING FOR SOMEWHERE TO SPEND THEIR ILL-GOTTEN GAINS

THEY HAD NO SCHOOL IN FENTON TOWN, BUT IT DIDN'T MATTER MUCH BECAUSE NOBODY UNDER SIXTEEN WAS ALLOWED INTO TOWN...

...AND SINCE LIVING TO A RIPE OLD AGE WAS UNLIKELY, THE WHOLE POPULATION OF FENTON TOWN WAS IN THE PRIME OF LIFE...

...WHICH NEVERTHELESS DIDN'T PREVENT THE UNDERTAKER FROM MAKING MONEY WITH ALMOST INSOLENT EASE...

...HE, LIKE ALL THE OTHER MERCHANTS IN THE TOWN, PAID A PERCENTAGE OF HIS TAKINGS TO DEAN FENTON...

ABANDONED BY THE PIONEERS WHO FOUNDED IT, THE BOOM TOWN HAD BEEN TAKEN OVER BY DEAN FENTON, A SCOUNDREL OF THE WORST KIND, WHO HELD HIS HEADQUARTERS IN THE 'QUEEN OF HEARTS' SALOON

SUCH SHERIFFS AS TRIED TO KEEP A SEMBLANCE OF ORDER IN FENTON TOWN WERE *SENT PACKING*...

...OR EVEN DID A MOONLIGHT FLIT WITHOUT WAITING FOR THE REMOVAL MEN...

...WHILE THE MAJORITY ADDED TO FENTON'S FORTUNE VIA THE UNDERTAKER'S COLLECTION SERVICE

THE ROULETTE WHEEL WAS FIXED...

37? THERE AIN'T 37 NUMBERS ON A ROULETTE WHEEL!

THERE ARE ON THIS ONE AN' I GOT A SEVEN-SHOOTER THAT SAYS SO!

THE DICE LOADED, THE CARDS MARKED...

I'M JUST HAVING A HAND OF PATIENCE TILL THE POKER CUSTOMERS ARRIVE

LOOKS GUOD! I SEE ALL THE ACES ARE THERE!

...THE WHISKY WATERED, THE FOOD TERRIBLE, AND THE PIANO OUT OF TUNE...

FIGHT?

NAW, HEARTBURN

...DESPITE ALL THIS, EVERY JOINT IN THE TOWN WAS FULL EXCEPT THE DISUSED JAIL...

...AND DEAN FENTON COUNTED UP EVERY NIGHT A PILE OF TAKINGS BIG ENOUGH TO STUFF A PIG

IT IS INTO THE MAIN STREET OF THIS GODLESS TOWN THAT WE NOW SEE RIDING A LONE HORSEMAN WHO'S A LONG WAY FROM HOME

4

5

6

7

8

I HEARD THE CLICK OF THE HAMMER. NEXT ONE TO TRY A TRICK LIKE THAT WON'T LIVE LONG ENOUGH TO BE SORRY

EVERYBODY OUT! I'M CLOSING THIS PLACE UP!

ALL THE INHABITANTS OF FENTON TOWN HAVE FLED. A TORRENTIAL DOWNPOUR HAS PUT OUT THE FIRE WHICH HAD PARTIALLY DESTROYED THE SALOON...

...AND THE TOWN HAS LOST NOT ONLY ITS NAME BUT ITS MASTER, HERDED OFF BENEATH A LOWERING SKY AS LUCKY LUKE'S PRISONER

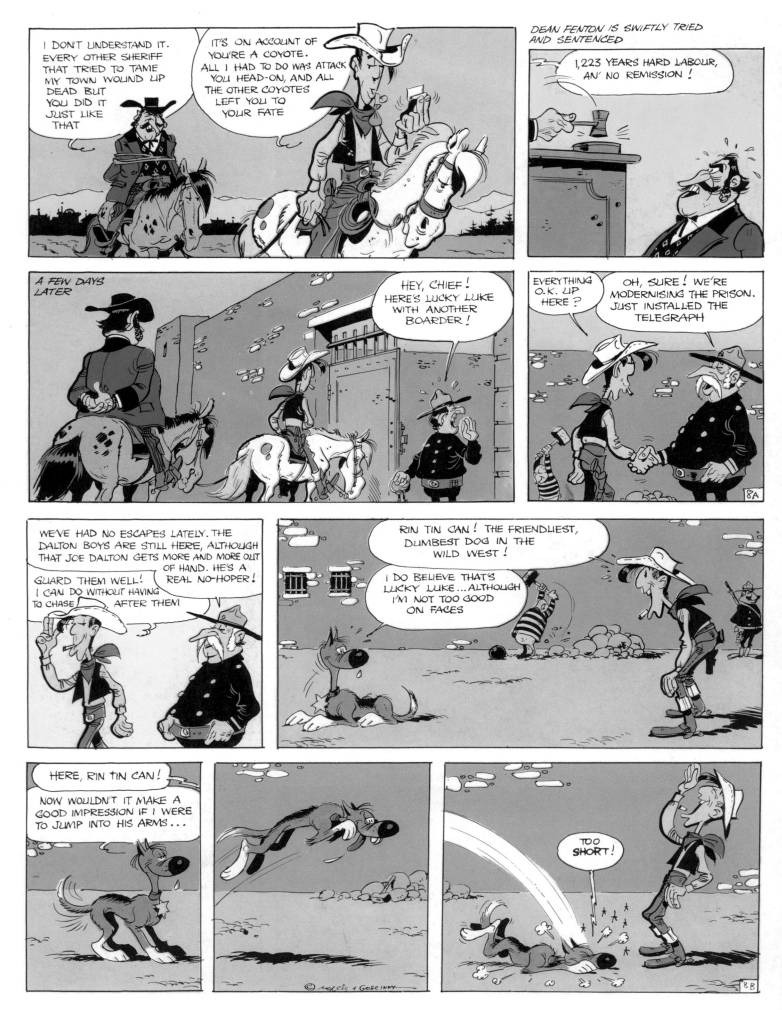

10

14

16

18

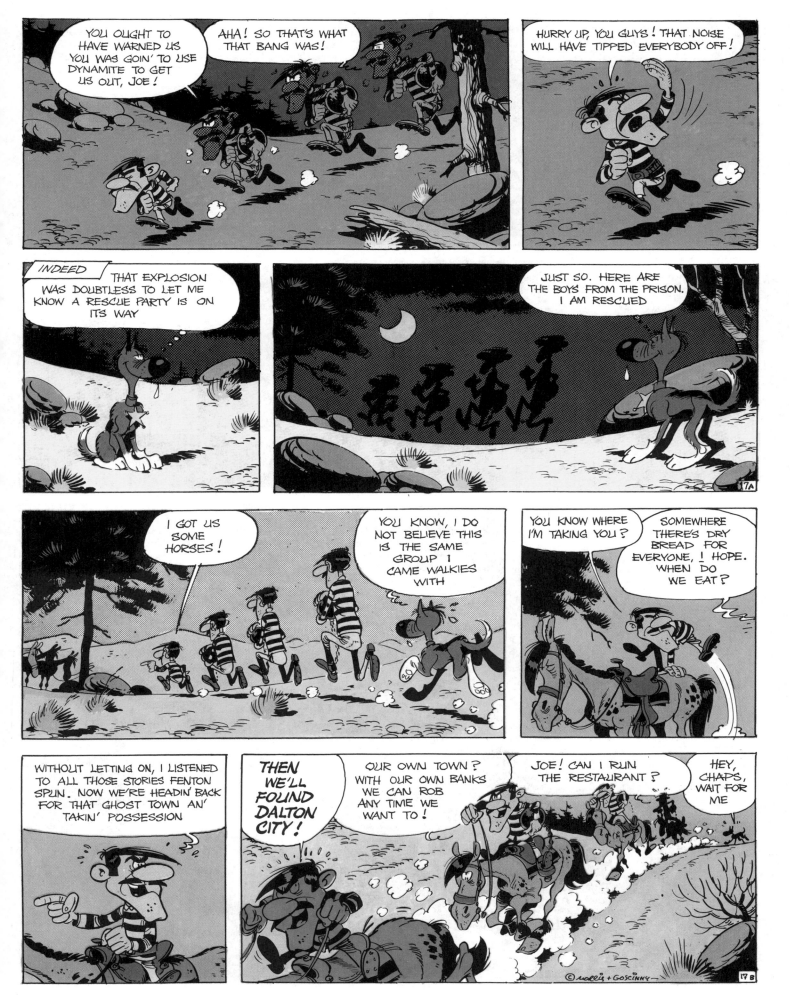

20

21

22

23

24

26

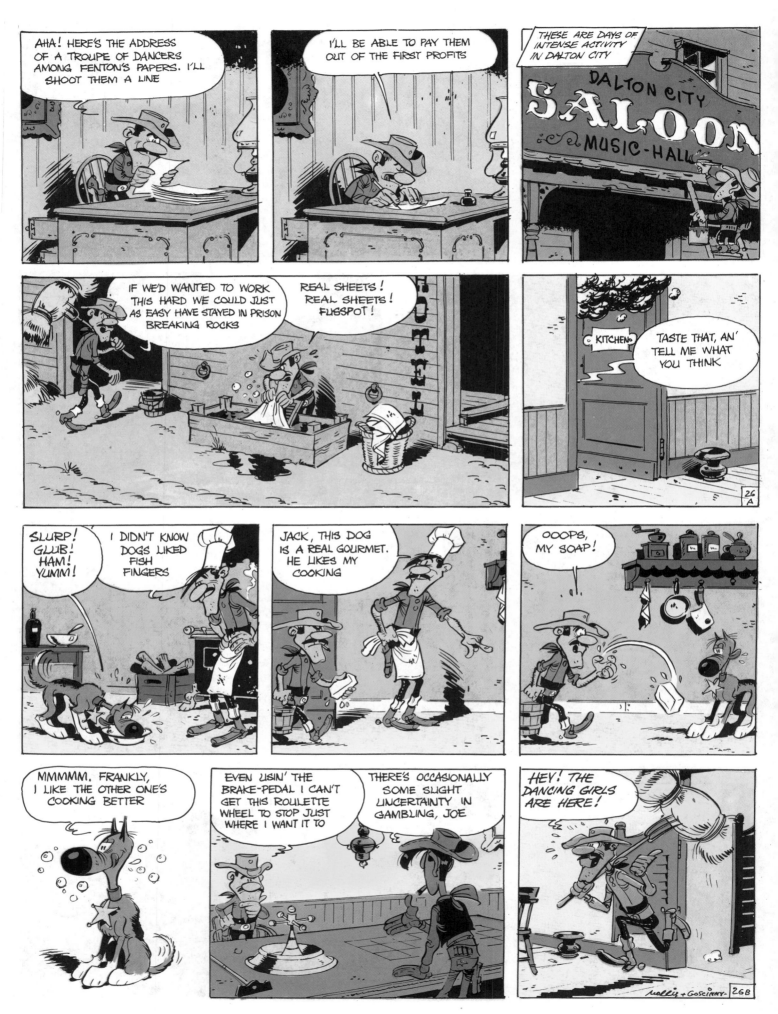

28

32

37

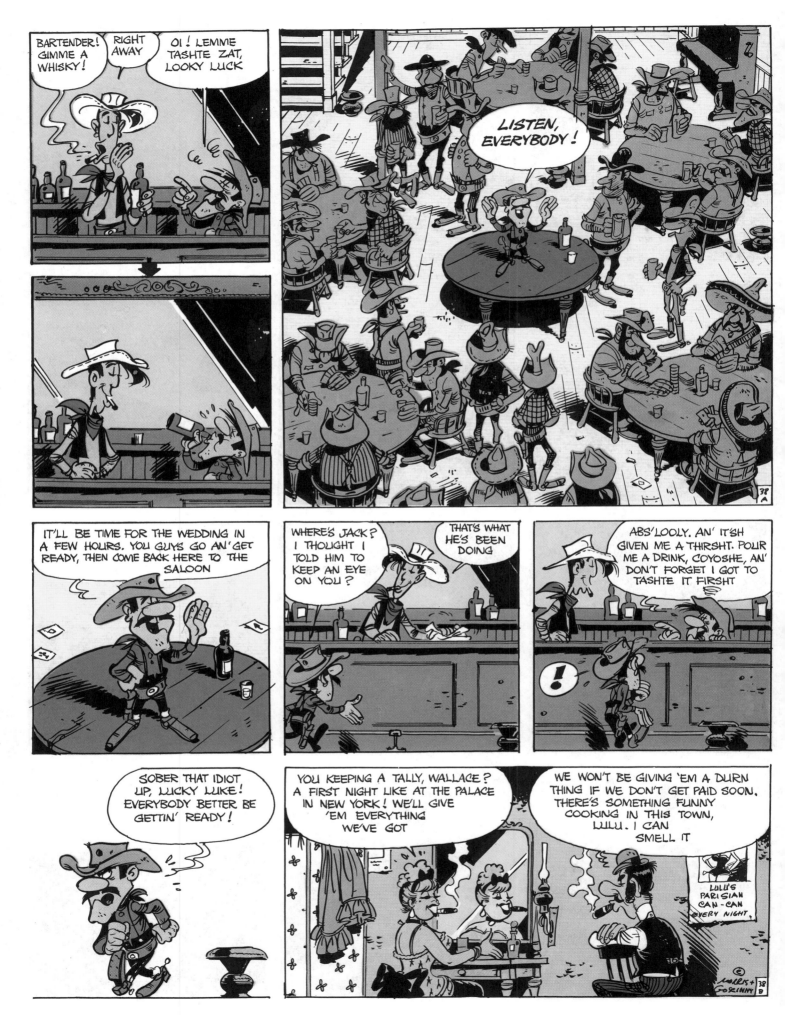

42

44

THE DALTON GANG

Left to right: Bill Power, Bob Dalton, Grat Dalton, Dick Broadwell.

The Dalton boys came from a family of 15 brothers and sisters born between 1852 and 1874 and were honest law abiding citizens . . . at the start. Frank Dalton was killed in 1887 while protecting Fort Smith as deputy marshal, and his brothers - Grat, Bob, Emmett and Bill - also became deputy marshals or posse members for the federal courts of their home state of Kansas.

However, they were eventually lured into crime. When not chasing outlaws in posses, Emmett was employed on a ranch as a cowboy and became acquainted with other outlaws - including Bill Power and Dick Broadwell pictured above - who were to become members of the Dalton Gang. At the same time, Bob and Grat began to get into trouble with their employers and were dismissed from their positions.

Bob, Grat and Emmett, with Dick Broadwell and Bill Power, formed the Dalton Gang, and were to become famous train robbers, continuously pursued by posse members alongside whom they had once ridden. The Gang held up numerous trains between February 1891 and July 1892, making away with thousands of dollars. Only Grat was once captured and sentenced, but he soon escaped from jail to join the others in their hideout.

The Dalton Gang decided to steal enough money to leave the country with one last big robbery. A plan was devised in 1892 - similar to the tale spun in Lucky Luke's 'The Outlaw' - to rob two banks in the same town at the same time, a feat no other gang had attempted. Regrettably, the Daltons chose their hometown of Coffeyville, Kansas and, despite wearing false beards, they were recognized by some of the citizens, who quickly took up positions to defend their town. A fierce gunfight took place in which four of the Gang and four of the townfolk died. Emmett was the only member to survive and was sentenced to life in prison. However, he was pardoned in 1907 by the Governor, and spent the rest of his life in California!

In the meantime, another brother, Bill Dalton, had trodden his own path of crime, first as a member of the Wild Bunch and later as the leader of his own gang. But, like his brothers, he too was gunned down following a bank robbery in 1894.

Sources: history.cc.ukans.edu/heritage and www.gunslinger.com